GALAXY ZACK

JOURNEY TO JUNO

By Ray O'Ryan

Illustrated by Colin Jack

LITTLE SIMON

New York   London   Toronto   Sydney   New Delhi

ABDO Spotlight

ABDOPUBLISHING.COM

Reinforced library bound edition published in 2015 by Spotlight, a division of ABDO, PO Box 398166, Minneapolis, Minnesota 55439. Spotlight produces high-quality reinforced library bound editions for schools and libraries. Published by agreement with Little Simon.

Printed in the United States of America, North Mankato, Minnesota.
042015
092015

**THIS BOOK CONTAINS
RECYCLED MATERIALS**

An imprint of Simon & Schuster Children's Publishing Division.
1230 Avenue of the Americas, New York, New York 10020
Copyright © 2013 by Simon & Schuster, Inc. All rights reserved, including the right of reproduction in whole or in part in any form. LITTLE SIMON is a registered trademark of Simon & Schuster, Inc., and associated colophon is a trademark of Simon & Schuster, Inc.

**LIBRARY OF CONGRESS
CATALOGING-IN-PUBLICATION DATA**

*This book was previously cataloged with the following
information:*

O'Ryan, Ray.
  Journey to Juno / by Ray O'Ryan ; illustrated by
Colin Jack. — 1st ed.
    p. cm. — (Galaxy Zack ; 2)
  Summary: On the planet Nebulon in 2120, Zack
joins his school's Explorers Club and visits Juno,
a planet made of crystals, but he is less than thrilled
when he is partnered with the class bully.
  ISBN 978-1-4424-5390-6 (pbk. : alk. paper) — ISBN 978-
1-4424-5391-3 (hardcover : alk. paper) — ISBN 978-1-4424-5392-0
(ebook)
  [1. Science fiction. 2. Explorers—Fiction. 3. Human-alien encounters—
Fiction. 4. Bullies—Fiction.] I. Jack, Colin, ill. II. Title.
PZ7.O7843Jo 2013
[Fic]—dc23
                          2012005691

978-1-61479-368-7 (reinforced library bound edition)

A Division of ABDO   abdopublishing.com

CONTENTS

Chapter 1
Play Ball!

Zack Nelson and his friend Drake Taylor sat in the home stadium of the Creston City Comets. A bright orange field spread out below them.

"Okay, Drake," Zack said. "I know I'm still the new kid on Nebulon. And I've never seen a galactic blast game

1

before, but I have one question: Where are the players?"

Drake smiled and pointed to both sides of the field.

Zack looked down and saw two teams of robots. Suddenly a whistle blew, and all the robots scrambled out onto the field.

"So people don't play galactic blast? Robots do?" Zack asked.

"The robots pitch and hit and run and field," explained Drake. "But people operate the robots using remote control units."

The game began. Zack was thrilled to see that galactic blast was played just like baseball back on Earth. He instantly understood the game.

A robot batter smacked the ball deep into the outfield. A robot outfielder made a diving catch.

"This is so cool," said Zack. "I've got to tell my friend Bert about this. We used to watch baseball together all the time back on Earth."

"Zack, would you like to share a bag of roasted nebu-nuts?" Drake asked. "They are my favorite snack at a galactic blast game. They are very crunchy."

"Sure!" Zack exclaimed. "My treat!"

Zack got up from his seat and hurried to the snack stand. He bought a big bag of roasted nebu-nuts.

"That will be two triptons, please," said the snack vendor.

Zack fished around in his pocket. He pulled out two square yellow coins.

"Thank you," he said, handing the coins to the vendor.

The nuts were warm and had a sweet, smoky smell.

Nebu-nuts look like peanuts, only they're much bigger and rounder, Zack thought.

When Zack returned to his seat, he was surprised to find another boy sitting there. Zack recognized the boy from his class. He was a Sprockets student named Seth Stevens.

"Oh, hi, Seth," Zack said. "You're sitting in my seat."

"Oh yeah, well it is *my* seat now!"
Seth shouted.

"But I was sitting there first," argued
Zack.

"Well, I am sitting here *now*, wimpy
Earthling!" Seth shot back.

"Come on, Zack," Drake said as he stood up. "Let us go and find other seats. I think I see some open seats by your dad."

What a bully, Zack thought. He followed Drake.

Zack and Drake found two empty seats a few rows away. Zack's dad was sitting nearby with some of his Nebulite friends. Dad smiled and waved at Zack and Drake.

"What's Seth's problem?" asked Zack as he sat down.

"Seth is the phase-two class bully," Drake explained. Phase two was Zack and Drake's grade in school. "He likes to give kids a hard time. Especially new kids."

Great, thought Zack. *That's just what I need.*

Chapter 2
Nebulon Navigators

The next day Zack floated through space. Whenever he saw a cool-looking planet, he dropped down for a visit.

One planet had giant trees that were more than a mile tall. Another planet had waterfalls that fell up, not down. Zack wished he could visit

every single planet in the galaxy.

"Zack?" said a soft voice that came drifting through space. "Zack Nelson?" the voice said, a little louder this time. "Can you please tell the class the answer to problem number seven?"

Zack looked up and realized that he was not in space at all. He was sitting in school, in Ms. Rudolph's class at Sprockets Academy. He had been daydreaming.

Zack scratched his head. "Forty-two?" he replied hopefully.

The whole class giggled.

"Zack, we are studying grammar at the moment, not math," Ms. Rudolph explained. "Please pay attention."

The rest of the morning dragged for Zack. Just before the sonic recess bell chimed, Ms. Rudolph made an announcement.

"Don't forget, the Sprockets Academy Explorers Club is going on a very special trip this week," she began. "The club will be going to Juno. It's not too late to sign up."

Wow! Zack thought. He had been reading all about Juno in the Space and Science section of the *Nebulon News*—the planet's online holographic newspaper. Juno had just been discovered. Zack really wanted to go there.

"Students who go on the trip will be helping the Nebulon Navigators explore this new planet," Ms. Rudolph explained.

Zack then slipped into another daydream. This time he was exploring Juno. He stepped into a cave and found pieces of old pottery.

"There must have been life here thousands of years ago," Explorer Zack announced to the scientists.

"Zack, this is the most amazing discovery ever," said the head of the Nebulon Navigators. "You will be famous!"

Zack imagined a series of z-mail news blasts. Each one had a giant headline:

ZACK NELSON MAKES MOST IMPORTANT DISCOVERY EVER!

ZACK NELSON INVITED TO JOIN NEBULON NAVIGATORS!

ZACK NELSON, BOY GENIUS!

The sonic recess bell suddenly chimed, and Zack snapped out of his daydream.

"Permission slips are up on the school's Sprocketsphere site.

20

Please have your parents sign them and zap them back to me," said Ms. Rudolph.

Everyone quickly rushed out of the classroom.

"Who are the Nebulon Navigators?" Zack whispered to Drake.

"They are the most famous space scientists on Nebulon," Drake explained. "They explore other planets."

"Cool," replied Zack. "I really want to go to Juno."

"Great," Drake said. "I am a member of the Sprockets Explorers Club. You should join."

"I will. That way we can explore the galaxy together and make great discoveries," said Zack.

"Not if I make them first, Earth wimp!" said Seth Stevens. Seth pushed past Zack and ran out into the play zone for recess.

Chapter 3
Torkus Dorkus

Zack and Drake stood just outside the play zone.

"Why does Seth have to do stuff like that?" Zack asked. "Why does he have to call me names? I can't help it if I'm not from Nebulon."

"Try not to let it bother you, Zack,"

Drake said. "Seth thinks he is better than everyone else."

"Why?" asked Zack.

"His father works at Nebulonics," Drake explained.

"But, so does mine," Zack pointed out.

"Yes, but Seth's dad invented the Torkus Magnus, the fastest bike on Nebulon."

"Torkus DORKus," mumbled Zack.

"What did you say?" asked Drake.

"Uh, never mind," said Zack. "So, is it even faster than *your* bike?" Zack had ridden Drake's cool super-fast Nebulon bike the day they met.

"Twice as fast!" Drake replied. "It will not even be in the stores until sometime next year. Of course, Seth already has one."

"That's still no reason to be so mean," Zack said.

Zack and Drake stood in line for the simulon course. The course was the most popular recess activity.

None of the hoops, ladders, hurdles, or barriers were real. They were all 3-D holographic images—pictures of objects that looked just like the real thing. But that didn't make it any less fun.

Zack's turn came. He dashed down a narrow path. Then he jumped up and over a blinking fence. Dropping

to the ground, he crawled through a long, winding tube.

"Done!" shouted Zack.

"Pretty good," Drake said, looking at his Galactic Standard watch. "Twenty-two seconds."

"Big deal," snarled Seth. "I did it in eighteen seconds. You Earthlings are so slow."

Zack tried his best to ignore Seth.

Chapter 4
Permission Granted!

Zack took the Sprockets Speedybus home from school. He couldn't wait to tell his parents about the Explorers Club and the trip to Juno.

When he got home, Zack's dog, Luna, was there to greet him.

"Hey there, Luna!" said Zack. He

kneeled down to pet her head.

Luna licked Zack's face. Her tail wagged happily.

"I'm glad to see you too, girl," Zack said. "Come on!"

Zack's mom, Shelly Nelson, was in the garage. She was setting up the family's old barbecue grill from Earth.

"What do you need *that* for, Mom?"
Zack asked. "Can't you just ask Ira to
cook whatever you like?"

Ira was the Nelson family's Indoor
Robotic Assistant. He was part of the
electrical, mechanical, computer, and
communications systems of the entire
house. Ira cooked all the Nelsons'

meals. He also took messages, announced visitors, and made sure the temperature in the house was always comfortable.

"I thought it would be fun to show our new Nebulite friends how we made food back on Earth," Mom explained. "So your father and I are having a barbecue party this weekend."

"Sounds like fun," said Zack. He realized that it was Monday.

The journey to Juno was scheduled for Thursday. "I'll be back by then."

"Back?" Mom asked, stopping what she was doing. "Back from where?"

"From the planet Juno!" Zack exclaimed. He couldn't hide his excitement.

"There's an Explorers Club at Sprockets. They are going to Juno later this week. Can I join, Mom? Can I? Drake's going. We'll be helping the Nebulon Navigators explore Juno!"

"That's great, Zack," Mom replied. "Of course you can go. I'm very glad that you found a school club you want to join. Dad and I will download the permission form and zap it back to the school."

"Yippee wah-wah!" said Zack. Mom gave him a hug before he rushed inside. When Zack entered the kitchen, a familiar voice greeted him.

"Welcome home, Master Just Zack,"
Ira said immediately. When Zack first
met Ira, he called Zack "Master Zack."
Zack told Ira that he didn't have to call
him "master"—"just Zack" was fine.
Since then, Ira had called him "Master
Just Zack."

Zack was used to it now. And he kind of liked it.

"Hi, Ira," replied Zack. "May I have some peanut butter cookies?"

"Certainly," said Ira.

A plate full of cookies popped out of a slot in the wall. Zack grabbed one and took a bite.

"You sure these are peanut butter cookies, Ira?" he asked.

"Actually, Master Just Zack, they are nebu-nut cookies," Ira explained. "Peanuts do not grow on Nebulon."

"These are pretty good," Zack said. "But peanut butter is my all-time fave!"

Zack grabbed a few more cookies and stepped into the elevator. The doors slid shut and he took off— sideways.

Chapter 5
Thoughts of Juno

The elevator sped through the house. The doors opened, and Zack stepped into his bedroom. He sat at his desk to do his homework.

But Zack couldn't concentrate.

I'm going to Juno!

It was all Zack could think about!

Zack had not been happy when he moved from Earth to Nebulon. He missed his friends. He missed familiar foods. But if the Nelsons hadn't come to Nebulon, Zack would not be going to explore Juno.

I'll finish my homework later, Zack thought. He ran back into the elevator and sped to the living room.

Zack flipped on the sonic cell monitor, the Nebulon version of television. He put on the galactic blast

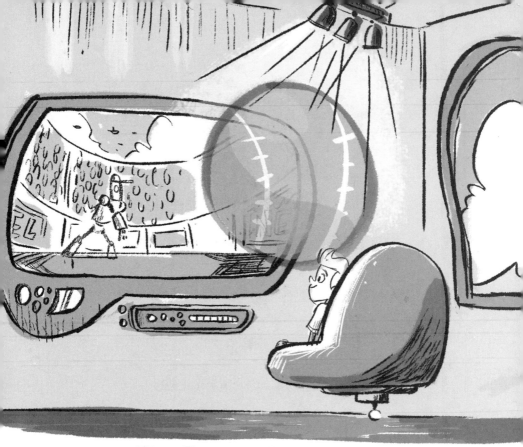

game. The Creston City Comets were
leading the Voltor Shocks 5 to 4.

A few minutes later, Zack's dad,
Otto Nelson, came home from his job
at Nebulonics.

"Hey, Captain!" Dad said. "How was school today?"

"Great!" Zack exclaimed. "I joined the Explorers Club. I'm going on a trip to Juno!"

"Wow! Got room for one more?" Dad joked.

Zack thought about Seth. "Dad, do you know the guy who invented the Torkus Magnus?" he asked.

"Of course! He's Fred Stevens, my
boss at Nebulonics. Remember—he
greeted us at the space station when
we first landed on Nebulon? I'm having
lunch with him tomorrow."

*Seth Stevens's dad is my dad's
boss!* Zack thought. *Ugh.*

"You like him?" Zack asked.

"Sure," Dad replied. "He's a great guy. Say, isn't Fred's son in phase two at Sprockets?"

"Yeah, I think he is," Zack muttered. "You know, I haven't met all the kids yet." Zack did not want to tell his dad what a big bully Seth was.

"Hi, Dad . . . ," said Charlotte and Cathy together. Zack's twin sisters often spoke as if they were one person.

"Look at what . . . ," Charlotte began.

". . . we got!" Cathy finished.

They squealed with delight. They held up identical pink dresses that had been sent from Earth.

"These are . . ."

". . . the coolest dresses ever!"

Then they ran off to their room to try the new dresses on.

Mom walked in with some laundry. "Hurry up, girls," she called after the twins. "It's almost time for dinner."

Zack and Dad went to watch the rest of the Comets game together, but only one thought filled Zack's mind.

I'm going to Juno!

Chapter 6
Juno Bound

Zack stood in front of Sprockets Academy. He wore his Explorers Club hat and his spacepack. Today he was going to Juno!

The rest of the club was gathered outside the school. Zack spotted Seth Stevens. Seth was the last person Zack hoped would be on this trip. Then he saw Drake.

"Drake, over here!" Zack called. Drake joined him.

"I cannot believe we are actually going to Juno," said Drake. "Only a handful of people have ever seen it."

A man stepped to the front of the crowd. He was tall and had a skinny green head. He had six long fingers on each hand.

On top of his thin head was a galactic blast cap that read DREXEL EXPLORERS CLUB EARTH JOURNEY 2098. Clearly this man was neither a Nebulite nor a human.

"Welcome, explorers!" he began. "I am Mr. Shecky, the adviser of the Sprockets Explorers Club. I'll be your leader on your journey to Juno. Now please follow me onto the space cruiser."

Zack, Drake, and the rest of the explorers piled onto a jumbo space cruiser.

A few moments later they took off into space.

Zack walked to a window to watch stars and comets streaking by.

"Hey—you're Zack, right?" asked Mr. Shecky, standing next to Zack.

Zack nodded.

"Ms. Rudolph told me about you,"
Mr. Shecky said. "She said that you're
from Earth, and that you're new on
Nebulon. Well, I'm from the planet
Drexel myself. I know what it's like to
be the new kid."

Zack pointed at Mr. Shecky's cap. "You've been to Earth?" he asked.

"Yup. I used to be a galaxy researcher," Mr. Shecky explained. "I was on the Drexel Deep Space Team. I love exploring planets. I moved to Nebulon to become the adviser for the Sprockets Academy Explorers Club."

Zack settled back into his seat and thought about the adventure ahead.

A short while later the cruiser began beeping. Everyone leaned forward.

"Attention, please. Arrival on Juno in five minutes. Prepare for landing," the cruiser said.

Zack looked out the window. He saw a craggy-looking planet that sparkled.

Juno looked as if it were covered in diamonds.

This is it! Zack thought.

The cruiser landed gently on the surface of Juno. The hatch opened and everyone stepped out. A sparkling crystal landscape stretched out before them.

Zack saw lots of space cruisers from other schools. They came from different planets, such as Zorba, Neptune, Cylon, and more.

Then Zack spotted the Nebulon Navigators team. They were already hard at work gathering samples.

"Wow! I can't believe I'm here with the Nebulon Navigators," Zack said to Drake.

"Welcome to Juno, everyone," Mr. Shecky announced. "Each school's Explorers Club has been assigned a section of Juno. Sprockets Academy will explore the southwest quadrant. Over there."

Mr. Shecky pointed to a series of caves in the distance.

"I'm going to break you into teams," said Mr. Shecky. "Everyone will work with a partner."

I hope Drake and I can be partners! thought Zack.

"You are to take notes, gather samples, record videos, and shoot photos with your team's handheld camtrams," Mr. Shecky continued.

Mr. Shecky began reading aloud pairs of names. When he got to Zack's name, Zack held his breath.

"'Zack Nelson and Seth Stevens!'" Mr. Shecky called out.

Oh no! Zack thought. *Not him!* He had a sinking feeling in the pit of his stomach.

Chapter 7
Crystal Caves

Zack and Seth set off for the crystal caves. *Okay, I'm not going to let Seth Stevens ruin my chance to explore Juno,* Zack thought.

Zack paused at the entrance to the first cave. He turned on his camtram and began recording. "This cave appears to be surrounded by a ring of flickering rocks," Zack reported. "It looks like they have tiny blinking lights inside them. Pretty cool, huh, Seth?" He figured he would at least try to get along with Seth.

But Seth had his face buried in his hyperphone.

"Yeah, yeah, whatever," mumbled Seth.

They stepped into the cave. The light from the camtram helped them see. Zack saw crystals of all shapes and sizes.

"Oh great!" Seth whined. "What kind of a dumb planet is this anyway? I can't even get z-mail service here. And I can't get on the Sprocketsphere to see what my friends are doing."

"But we're here to explore," Zack pointed out.

"Wrong!" Seth snapped. "*You* are here to explore. *I* am here to get famous for what you discover. So you better find something special."

Zack just shook his head.

"Hey, Earth wimp, get a picture of that!" shouted Seth. He pointed at a large crystal right over their heads.

Zack glanced up and saw what looked like an octopus hanging from the ceiling. He aimed the camtram and took a picture.

Zack and Seth walked deeper into the cave. They soon came to a river flowing through the icy crystal floor.

"Check out the colors!" said Zack Looking into the river, Zack saw tiny ribbons of color flowing through the water. "It's like a liquid rainbow."

"Just take a picture of it!" Seth said impatiently. "How am I going to get famous if you do not get proof of everything I discovered?"

Part of me doesn't even want to record any more discoveries, Zack thought. Not if Seth is going to take all the credit when I'm doing all the work.

"Why did you join the Explorers Club if you aren't even interested in exploring?" Zack asked Seth.

Seth shrugged. "My dad made me. He said it would look good on my student record."

Zack sighed. He pointed the camtram at the river and started recording it.

"All the colors of the rainbow seem to flow through this river," he said.

"Because we're in a cave, the colors can't be formed by sunlight. They are already in the water."

Seth quickly lost interest in what Zack was doing. He wandered over to the entrance of the cave. Then he pulled out his hyperphone and tried again to get a signal.

Zack hiked deeper into the cave. He went around a bend and found a pile of crystals.

Zack picked up one of the crystals. It felt smooth and cold.

Suddenly, Zack felt a wave of warm energy wash over him.

"Whoa. That heat is coming from the pile of crystals," Zack said.

He spotted a soft green glow coming from the pile. Zack moved a few crystals out of the way.

"It's a glowing green crystal!" he said. Then he quickly looked back over his shoulder to see if Seth was there.

Zack picked up the green crystal. Unlike the others, this one was warm. It was about the size of a baseball.

Zack opened his spacepack and slipped the crystal in.

"Seth is *not* going to take credit for this one!"

Chapter 8
An Amazing Discovery

Zack hurried back toward the cave entrance.

I'll show the green crystal to the other Explorers Clubs, he thought. *And maybe even to the Nebulon Navigators. I'll be famous!*

Once again Zack imagined a series

of news blasts. In his mind, giant z-mail headlines flooded Nebulon:

ZACK NELSON FINDS RAREST CRYSTAL EVER!

BOY EXPLORER MAKES GALAXY-SHAKING DISCOVERY!

ZACK NELSON AWARDED THE ZURBIC PRIZE FOR SCIENCE!

Zack rejoined Seth outside the cave.

"Come on!" said Seth. "There are more great

ZACK NELSON AWARDED THE ZURBIC PRIZE FOR SCIENCE!

discoveries for me to make."

Zack spent a few more hours recording interesting crystal and water formations. Seth spent the time complaining and pacing around. Then the two rejoined the rest of the Sprockets students.

Zack saw many students from different Explorers Clubs. They were all eagerly sharing the exciting discoveries they had made.

Seth grabbed the camtram right out of Zack's hands.

"Hey, everyone, check out all the grape stuff I found," said Seth.

"Grape?" Zack whispered to Drake.

"On Nebulon, we call awesome stuff 'grape,'" Drake explained. "It is like when people on Earth say 'cool.'"

Seth played back the video and photos of all the discoveries that Zack had made. Everyone oohed and aahed as Seth took credit for all of Zack's hard work.

That's it! Zack thought. *I've had enough of Seth.*

"Thank you, Seth," said Mr. Shecky. "Excellent work."

Then Zack pulled the green crystal from his spacepack. It glowed and pulsed with warm energy.

"Mr. Shecky, I also found this," Zack announced.

Mr. Shecky's eyes opened wide.

"Zack, where did you find this?" He gasped. "Do you know what this is?"

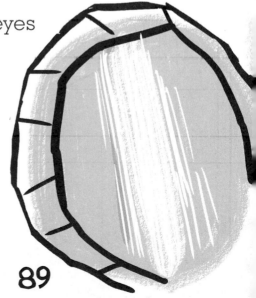

89

"No, I don't," Zack replied.

Seth glared at Zack.

"That, young man, is a galaxy gemmite!" exclaimed Mr. Shecky. "That crystal has an incredible amount of energy stored within it. Usually they're the size of pebbles.

But a gemmite this size could power all of Creston City for a whole year. A gemmite this large hasn't been found in more than one hundred years!"

Seth clenched his fists. His face turned bright red.

Zack smiled. *Maybe now more kids will like me*, he thought.

A researcher from the Nebulon Navigators hurried over to the Sprockets group.

"What is all the fuss about, Mr. Shecky?" the researcher asked.

Zack held up the gemmite.

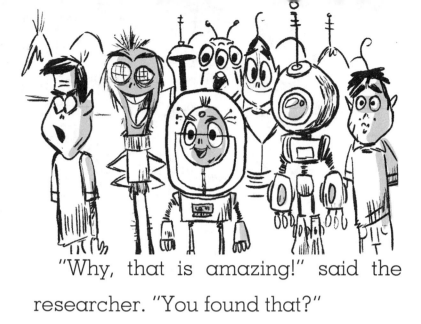

"Why, that is amazing!" said the researcher. "You found that?"

Zack nodded.

"No fair!" cried one the Explorers Club members.

"Yeah!" shouted another member. "We have all been in the Explorers Club longer than Zack. We have been on lots more trips. We never found anything like that!"

Oh no! Zack thought. *This is not what I wanted to happen!*

As the excitement increased, more Explorers Clubs came over to see what was going on. So did the rest of the Nebulon Navigators.

"A huge gemmite!" exclaimed one of the Navigators. "Who found this?"

Zack stepped forward.

"The students of the Sprockets Academy Explorers Club found it," Zack announced. "We make a great team!"

Everyone in the club cheered. They all surrounded Zack and patted him on the back.

Everyone except Seth, who looked on from a distance.

Chapter 9
Fame and Friendship

Zack had a great time on the trip back to Nebulon. Everyone on the space cruiser was in a fantastic mood.

The Explorers Club was proud of the incredible discovery they had made. And they were happy that Zack shared the credit with everyone.

Zack finally began to feel like he belonged on Nebulon.

When he got home, Zack was shocked to see how fast the news of his discovery had spread. Z-mail blasts were everywhere showing the Sprockets Explorers Club holding the gemmite. Zack was up front in all the photos.

Zack and his family gathered in the living room. He flipped on the sonic cell

monitor. The *Evening Galactic News* came on.

"Good evening. A group of students from Nebulon has made an amazing discovery," the newscaster said. "The Explorers Club of Sprockets Academy found the largest gemmite anyone has seen in years."

Charlotte and Cathy both pointed at the screen.

"Look . . ."

". . . it's Zack!" they both said.

"We're very proud of you, Zack," said Dad. "You're a natural explorer!"

Zack's mom watched all the kids on Juno celebrating with Zack.

"And it looks like you made some new friends," said Mom.

Just then Zack's video-chat hyperphone started buzzing. He looked at the screen.

"It's Bert calling from Earth," Zack said. "I'll be in my room!"

"Go ahead, Captain," said Dad. "We'll just watch you on the sonic cell monitor!"

Zack hurried to his room. He plugged the hyperphone into his 3-D holocam.

Instantly a life-size 3-D image of Bert appeared in his room.

"Dude, I just saw you on TV," Bert said. "You're famous!"

Zack was still amazed at how lifelike the image of his friend was. It felt like Bert was right there hanging out in his room—just like in the old days back on Earth.

"It was pretty grape finding that gemmite," admitted Zack.

"'Grape'?" asked Bert. "Are you hungry?"

"No!" Zack laughed. "Sorry—that's what they say on Nebulon when something is cool," he explained.

"Sounds like you're fitting right in there," said Bert.

"I'm doing okay," Zack said. "But I still

miss hanging out with you."

Zack went to pat Bert on the back. But no matter how lifelike the image of Bert was, it still was not the real thing. His hand passed right through the 3-D image of his friend!

"Whoa, dude. That is just *too* creepy!" said Zack.

Chapter 10
Burgers and Dogs

A couple of days later the Nelsons held their old-fashioned Earth-style barbecue. They had invited all their new Nebulite friends.

Zack and the girls helped Mom carry platters of uncooked burgers, hot dogs, chicken, corn on the cob,

and vegetables out to the backyard.

"Hey, look what we got!" shouted Dad. He ran from the house holding an open package. "Real peanut butter cookies, made with real peanuts!"

"Wow!" exclaimed Zack. "Where'd these come from?"

"Bert's mom made them," Dad said. "Bert told her how much you missed real peanut butter cookies—"

"Excuse me, Mr. Nelson," Ira said. "Some of your guests have arrived."

A few minutes later a crowd of Nebulites gathered in the backyard. Zack didn't know the adults, but he recognized most of the kids from school.

And of course Drake was there. The kids all gathered around the barbecue grill.

"Yow! What are those burning round things?" Drake asked.

"Those are burgers," explained Zack. "They're yumzers!"

"Mr. Stevens and his family have arrived," Ira announced.

Dad's boss, Fred Stevens, walked into the backyard. He was followed by

his wife, Angie, and their son, Seth.

Seth Stevens! Zack thought. *Here in my yard? I guess I should be polite since he's my guest.*

Zack walked up to Seth.

"Hi, Seth. Glad you made it. Would you like some food?"

Just then Luna ran over. She jumped up onto Seth.

"Yah!" Seth cried, backing away in fear.

Zack was surprised to see Seth so scared. Despite all the bullying, Zack actually felt sorry for Seth.

Zack remembered how frightened Drake had been the first time he met Luna.

"Luna's friendly," Zack told Seth. "She won't hurt you. She's my dog."

Seth joined the other kids over near the food.

"Would you like a hot dog?" Zack offered.

"You eat dogs?" Seth said. "But I thought you liked Luna."

"Hot dogs aren't made from dogs," Zack explained. "That's their name."

"Weird," said Seth.

"Would anyone . . ."

". . . like to . . ."

". . . dance?" Charlotte and Cathy asked.

The Nebulites looked puzzled.

"You know . . . dancing," added Zack's mom.

"Ira, how about a little dance music?" Zack's dad said.

"Certainly, Mr. Nelson," said Ira.

Loud dance music blared out into the backyard.

Zack's dad and mom started to dance. Their Nebulite guests just stared at them. Music and dancing were not popular on Nebulon.

Mr. Shecky joined right in. "I love music!" he said. "Come on, everybody. It's fun!"

Slowly a few Nebulites joined in. They imitated the moves that Zack's dad and mom were making.

Zack turned away, trying not to giggle. He glanced over at all his new Nebulite friends. He thought about his adventure on Juno. Seth wasn't even bothering him today! He smiled and looked up into the pink Nebulon sky.

That's when Zack saw something streak across the sky.

What is that? Zack wondered.

Zack rushed inside. He hurried to his room and flipped on his überzoom galactic telescope. He zoomed in on the streak. Now he could clearly see a body and wings. Zack could not believe his eyes.

TO BE CONTINUED . . .